Walt Disney World
FLORIDA

PLUTO
and the Adventure
of the Golden Scepter

GOLDEN PRESS
Western Publishing Company, Inc.
Racine, Wisconsin

Morty Mouse threw a stick high into the air. With a happy bark, Pluto ran and caught it before it touched the ground.

"Here comes another one," called Morty. But then he stopped, letting the stick drop from his hand. They had been playing in the courtyard of Cinderella's Castle, and now, from deep within the castle, they could hear the sound of someone crying.

Puzzled, Morty and Pluto slipped through the
mighty archways and up a shadowy, winding stairway. The stairway led them into the throne room,
where they found the King. He was very unhappy
because his golden scepter was missing.

"A king *must* have a scepter!" he cried. "It is the thing that shows he is the king. I can't hold court without it." He sadly shook his head.

"Don't worry," said Morty. "Pluto is good at find-
ing things. You'll track it down, won't you, boy?"

Much to Morty's surprise, Pluto lowered his head
and looked worried.

"Perhaps he doesn't know what a scepter is," suggested the King.

"Well," said Morty, "it looks like a stick, and you know what a stick is, Pluto."

"Only it isn't a stick," added the King.

Find a stick that isn't a stick! thought Pluto. Well, he certainly would try. Out of the castle he ran, with Morty close behind.

On Main Street, Pluto looked for a stick that might be the King's scepter. *Perhaps this is it,* he thought as he picked up something from a bench.

"Put that down, Pluto!" scolded Mickey Mouse. He was dressed in a bright red uniform with shiny brass buttons. "That's the baton that I use to lead the band."

"We're looking for the King's scepter, Mickey," explained Morty.

"Well, why don't you look in Liberty Square?" suggested Mickey, and away he marched, waving his baton.

Pluto hurried on.

"Nine o'clock and all is well!" called Donald Duck, Liberty Square's town crier.

Then he changed his mind.

"Five minutes *after* nine, and all is *not* well!" he sputtered as Pluto tried to pull his walking stick away from him. Poor Pluto had made another mistake.

And it wasn't his last!

In Tomorrowland, what he thought was the scepter turned out to be the riding crop Minnie Mouse carried. Minnie was a tour guide, and she held the crop high in the air so that visitors were able to follow her more easily.

Later, Pluto was certain Goofy was holding the
scepter—until Morty explained it was a stick used for
picking up scrap paper.

And when Pluto tried to grab the Fairy God-mother's magic wand, she almost turned him into a pumpkin. Morty hastily apologized for him, and they hurried on their way once more.

They had searched nearly all of Walt Disney World
when, tired and discouraged, they finally came to
Adventureland.

"It's no use," admitted Morty. "We've failed. The
King will be very disappointed."

"I don't know what's troubling you fellows," said
a friendly voice, "but I'm sure a jungle cruise will
cheer you up."

Wearily, Morty and Pluto followed the jungle explorer-guide to an Adventureland boat. It was clear, however, that Morty had little interest in the ride as their boat started down the winding river. He didn't even look up as the jungle closed in, surrounding them with trees and with jungle sounds—monkeys chattering, lions growling, elephants trumpeting—and a dog barking.

"A dog barking? *That* isn't a jungle sound!" said Morty, looking around in surprise.

The barking dog was Pluto. And the reason he was
barking was that he had found the golden scepter at
last! There on the riverbank stood an elephant. His
trunk was firmly wrapped around the scepter, and he
was using it as a back scratcher!

Morty could hardly believe his eyes.

"How did you get that scepter?" he demanded.

"I flew into the castle and found it lying on a table," a voice answered. The voice came from a red, blue, and green parrot in a nearby tree. "My elephant friend was so hot and dusty that he needed it, and so I got it for him."

"But the King needs that scepter, too," said Morty.
"You shouldn't have taken it."

"And how would you suggest that my good friend
remain comfortable here in this jungle?" retorted the
parrot, ruffling his feathers. It was clear that he was
ready to argue all day.

Suddenly Morty noticed that Pluto was pointing upstream and whispering something to the elephant. Much to the surprise of Morty and the parrot, the elephant gave Pluto the scepter and splashed eagerly into the river and began to swim away.

The pilot of the jungle boat turned his craft around and followed the elephant. He was curious to see what would happen. Soon they came to a spot where a waterfall tumbled and splashed over rocks, making a giant-sized shower bath. Pluto had noticed this spot from the boat, and he knew it was just the thing for a hot, dusty elephant.

And the elephant? Why, he enjoyed that shower so much that he stayed there ever after. (He is now the most contented elephant—and the cleanest, too—in the whole jungle.)

Morty was delighted as he followed Pluto up the stairs of Cinderella's Castle to return the scepter. And the King was even more delighted to receive it. But proudest and happiest of all was Pluto—for, as his first official act of the day, and in recognition of the great service Pluto had performed, the King dubbed Pluto a Royal Knight of the Golden Scepter!